This book belongs to

_____

_____

Cari

WHO'S TAKEN IT?

Written and illustrated by
Andrew Green

Published by AGB&I Ltd
First published 2018

ISBN: 978-1-9999507-0-5

THIS WAY
TO THE JUNGLE

FOR CARLY,
JOE, ELLIOT
AND CHARLES X

"Oh NO, that's not funny!" Sebastian cried.
"The loo roll's been taken from right by my side!"

"Where **IS** it? Who's **GOT** it? Please, please bring it back!
I'm going to be late for my mid-morning snack!"

"I'm sorry," hissed Solomon,
"don't look at me!
Hey Sanjay, can **you** tell him
where it might be?"

"I would if I could
but can't see very well.
I've misplaced my glasses,
try asking Chantelle!"

"There's no loo roll here but I wish you success!
Try Billy the lion or Tess the lioness."

"Well **somebody's** got it,
please be a kind bunch!
I'm hungry, I'm going
to miss out on lunch!"

"How very mischievous! Who'd do such a thing?
Hey monkeys, did you see, up there on your swing?"

"Wee hee!"
said the monkeys.

"Not US sir! No WAY!

But Hannah is down there, can SHE save the day?"

"No sign of it! Oh I feel sorry for you!
It can't be much fun being stuck on the loo!"

"Squawk! SQUAWK! We've been busy
rehearsing our show!
Excuse me Sam Sloth, can you help?
Do you know?"

"I'm really quite dozy, I've not seen a peep.

Try Zelda, now please let me go back to sleep."

"I'm sorry,
I've only got undies and socks!
I hope that you find it,
perhaps try the crocs."

"Where is it? Who's got it?
Oh where can it be?
I really don't want
to skip afternoon tea!"

"Re**lax** Seb,
don't worry,
there's help in the air!

Can Imogen find it?
She'll see from up there!"

"No use, I can't find it,
I've scanned all around!
The meerkats might have it,
down there on the ground."

"We **promise** we haven't, we've played here all day!
Hey rhinos, do you two have something to say?"

"I can't be too sure, but I think I can see
Tobias with something up there near his tree!"

Sebastian shouted,

"Whoever you are, just why did you take it? It's very bizarre!

I've got a sore bottom, my legs really ache!

But if it's returned, I'll forgive your mistake!"

"Oh GREAT,

now it's raining - I hope you are near!

I'm getting all wet, sitting here on my rear!

"Before I get cross, you should bring it to me!

I'm going to count slowly one, two...

... three!"

Andrew Green is a children's writer and illustrator from the UK,
and works from a small studio in his garden.

"It's full of spiders, but they pay their rent by helping with artwork or scaring off flies."

If you would like to see more of Andrew Green's work, please visit
www.andrewgreenart.co.uk

39870643R00020

Made in the USA
Middletown, DE
20 March 2019